The Waitress, the Whiskey & the Handcuffs

Les Becker

DEDICATION

For Ruby – the "Real" one.

CONTENTS

FORWARD

The Waitress, the Whiskey and the Handcuffs is the first in a series of novellas entitled "The Ruby Chronicles".

Ruby is a real person – a close friend of the author, Les Becker, who Les affectionately refers to as her "Little Ol' Landlady". Although no longer her tenant, Les still visits Ruby on a regular basis, sharing life, love and laughter. She considers Ruby to be much more than a friend; she is family.

"The Ruby Chronicles" are fictional stories loosely based on incidents and anecdotes told to the author in general conversation, and have been written up in an entertaining format with Ruby's express permission. These stories should never be considered in any way, shape or form to be an expression of the actual life of the person behind the caricature of Ruby Daniel.

PART I: THE WAITRESS

In 1957, Ruby was a 30-something waitress/barmaid/short-order cook in an out-of-the-way backwoods tavern down a side road off the highway. She was also the bookkeeper, the housekeeping staff and the bouncer, although she didn't get paid extra for any of those tasks - there was just no one else to do them. It may not have been fair, but a job was a job, and she had kids to support. She kind of enjoyed the bouncing duties, anyhow.

Ruby never would have used the term 30-something to describe herself. She would be much more likely to say, "Mind your own birthdays," if asked her age by any of the ne'er-do-wells that frequented the place, which was so far back in the sticks that it didn't even have a name. Everybody called it The

Dump, because if you drove another quarter mile down the side road, the town garbage dump is where you finished up.

Ruby had lived a fairly decent life up to becoming employed at The Dump. She'd married a little on the late side, if 25 could be considered late, but at least she'd married. Her husband bought a small chicken farm up the North Side Road after the war, and asked Ruby to marry him the very same day. Roy had seen her to a few dances over the years, and written from overseas, but Ruby hadn't really ever considered him to be a serious suitor. His proposal came out of the blue. Ruby asked for a day or two to think it over.

There wasn't much to think over, really, when it came right down to it. She'd known Roy all her life. She knew he was a hard-working man and she doubted he'd run around. His was certainly the first proposal she'd received, and she wondered if there would ever be another if she turned him down. The practical side of her realized that they were a "good match", as her mother would say (and did), and there wasn't much of a romantic side of Ruby to contradict the idea, anyhow. When Roy returned for her answer, she accepted his proposal and cooked him the first of many suppers while they worked out the arrangements.

Chicken farming didn't turn out to be as lucrative as Roy had hoped. By the time the two kids were in school, he had taken a job driving truck on the city run for Fulton Berries, the only hothouse strawberry growers in the district, so at least he was employed year 'round. It meant Ruby had to run the farm on her own through the week while Roy was away, but they got by all right - until Roy crashed his truck one Christmas and killed himself in the process.

Ruby, ever practical, moved her mother in to help with the kids, and took the weekend job at The Dump before Roy was in the ground a month. The first shift she worked was the first time she'd set foot in such a place, but she got used to it fast. Chicken farming was harder work than beer-slinging. She still ran the farm mostly on her own, and generally missed Roy most when she had to do the slaughtering. It was a messy job, killing chickens, and bouncing drunks was more enjoyable.

The Dump was open on Friday and Saturday nights,

from 7 pm until Ruby managed to shovel the last drunk out the door, which was usually close to 4 am Saturday morning, but only about 1 or 2 am on any given Sunday, because nobody dared miss church in the morning. Those that were married didn't want to deal with their wives (and mothers-in-law); those who considered themselves lucky to have avoided that ball-and-chain didn't want to deal with the married gents - it was on their farms and in their businesses in town that most of the single fellas earned their livings. The rest lived and worked in "the bush" clearing timber Monday through Friday, and usually only got into town at all on the weekends, but they still went to church. Church was where the single girls were on Sunday.

The only three men in town to avoid services without guilty consciences on a Sunday morning were the same three that made Ruby clench her jaw and grit her teeth the most when they walked into The Dump. Two were the loudest, and the most obnoxious, and all three were the only ones she didn't dare try to bounce.

The biggest, loudest, and most boorishly obnoxious of the three was a cop - and a district officer to boot. The little spot on the highway called "Town" was too small for a police department of its own, along with all the other little blips up and down the line that also called themselves "Town", so the district was responsible for policing the whole string of them, all dotted along the highway from the big city in the East to the one in the West, and, with government-like lofty wisdom, the great minds in charge of the district decided that Judd Gulley should be the big arm of the law over several of the little towns between those two points. Judd was also the owner of The Dump, and therefore, Ruby's boss.

Wally McDonald was Judd's best buddy, and they might as well have been joined at the hip. Wally had never worked a day in his life, and Judd thought that was just fine. Wally rode shotgun in Judd's cruiser every shift, and when Judd was off work, he unstuck the cherry from the roof and Wally rode shotgun while the cruiser was just a plain ol' sedan.

The third guy that Ruby didn't dare bounce was Wilson Jones. He was "no higher than here," as Ruby would say, holding her hand level just below her bust, and considered not quite right.

"In the head, that is," Ruby would say. "Not stupid,

exactly, but… well, he don't even look right, if you catch my drift."

Wilson was known around town as "The Little Drunk". He was a logger, and a good one, by all accounts, in spite of his size, and shy as all get-out, probably because of it. He came out of the bush on Friday night, cash in hand, and he'd spend every cent of his week's wages on booze by the time he crawled back in on Sunday night. He very rarely spoke, drunk or sober, and when he did, he didn't make much sense. Not quite right.

For some reason, Judd Gulley took a shine to The Little Drunk, and Ruby was told that every third drink she brought him was on the house. Ruby told Judd he was an idiot.

"I know he's an idiot, but that's what you'll do."

"I mean *you're* an idiot, Judd Gulley," Ruby shot back, but she did as she was told. She wasn't to charge The Little Drunk for his meals, either, and since she had to cook those meals, that burned her even more than giving him free booze.

Worst of all, Judd kept a room upstairs for The Little Drunk to pass out in on Friday and Saturday nights (free of charge, of course), and it was up to Ruby to keep the linen clean. And dang, if the Little Drunk wasn't a bed-wetter.

The first time she'd had to change those sheets, she hadn't thought too much of it. Accidents do happen, especially where drunks lie down, and God knew she'd changed her share of pissy beds in her lifetime. But when the bed was wet the following day, too, she gave Judd what-for. For the life of him, Judd couldn't understand what her problem was.

"He don't give the room a chance to air before he stinks it up again, Judd, that's the problem!" Ruby complained. "That mattress is ruined, if it don't get a chance to dry before he pisses all over it a third time!"

"Well, whad'ya want me to do about it?! Throw on some cornstarch and flip it over," Judd laughed. Wally, the skunk, laughed right along with him, and Ruby wanted to bash their heads together. This conversation took place on a Monday morning, the first chance she had managed to run into Judd, and it happened right out on Main Street. Ruby stood on the sidewalk, face-on with Judd and Wally in the cruiser, with seemingly every old maid in town chancing by to cluck her tongue. Ruby was livid.

"There's only two sides to a mattress, Judd Gulley, and the next time Wilson Jones wets the bed, that mattress will be in the parking lot!" And that's where she dragged it, the following Saturday afternoon, and left it there, soggy and stinking to high Heaven, for Judd to find when he pulled into the parking lot.

"That'll fix The Little Drunk," Ruby thought.

But, Judd just laughed, and Wally along with him, and the two of them roped the mattress to the bumper of Judd's sedan and dragged it further down the side road to that other dump. And when Ruby went into The Little Drunk's room the next afternoon, she found an honest-to-God straw tick on the bedsprings; something she hadn't seen since she was a kid. Worse, it was wet, and the smell of urine mixed with dirty straw dang near made her upchuck.

She threw some corn starch on it, opened the window, and an hour later went back up and flipped the tick over. She knew, too, that next Sunday afternoon would see her dragging it out back and emptying the straw, to wash the burlap. But she'd be danged if she'd stuff a new tick. If Judd Gulley didn't see fit to cut straw, The Little Drunk could sleep on bare springs for all she cared.

If Ruby had known what was going to happen two years later, she'd likely have seen fit to cut straw herself, after all. As it was, she wished she'd had the sense to quit that God-awful job before the Whiskey games started…

PART II: THE WHISKEY

Ruby had got into a comfortable rut, between working the chicken farm and running The Dump on the weekends. The farm was doing well, considering she had more chickens than she could reasonably deal with herself, and yet she still couldn't afford to hire help.

The kids, surprisingly, were more than willing to deal with gathering eggs and cleaning coops, and her mother, even more surprisingly, took over the slaughtering tasks. She was very efficient, and once told Ruby that she enjoyed it immensely.

Ruby was shocked, and asked her mother how it was possible to actually enjoy killing chickens, especially considering the mess and noise involved with the sheer numbers of doomed birds being dealt with. Her mother shocked her even more with her explanation. She laughed - an evil, disconcerting kind of laugh, Ruby thought - before she replied.

"I don't mind saying, Ruby, that there's a lot of people over the years that have ticked me off to no end," she said, and went on to say that while she was busy with the "wet-work", as she called it, she was actually imagining all the people she held grudges against, in place of the chickens.

She would sling each bird over the chopping block and stretch its neck before cutting its head off with the small axe Ruby kept for this purpose. Then she would set the decapitated chicken back on its feet and it would strut away, spouting blood. The next in line would be walking around headless, too, before the first one fell over.

"I like to see how many I can get dancing at a time," she told Ruby, laughing that evil-sounding laugh again. "I had eight or nine going at once, last time. I'm getting faster."

Ruby was aghast, and never spoke to her mother about the slaughtering details again. It was bad enough knowing what she was thinking now during the "wet-work", since Ruby still had to be around for the rest of the business of the slaughtering.

The dead chickens would be gathered up and their feet tied together, and then hung upside down to finish draining. Once drained of blood, the birds were dunked into boiling water to make the plucking easier. When that was done, Ruby gratefully left the side yard.

Her mother did the actual cleaning of the chickens; Ruby couldn't stomach it, especially after learning about her mother's vivid imagination.

She kept her weekend job at The Dump partly because the farm was only large enough to generate enough eggs and poultry to sell in the immediate area, and partly because every time she tried to quit, Judd Gulley would give her a raise. Every small stipend made it a little easier to decide that she could stick it out among the drunks, but it was never long before it came to where some idiot would do something to make her want to quit again. Most times, the idiot was Judd Gulley, himself. Take the "whiskey games", for example…

Judd kept a barrel of swish in the back store-room, along with the regular barrels of not-so-high-class whiskey he bought from a local bootlegger, and the cases of beer. Judd was nothing, if not cheap, and selling bootleg whiskey saved, or rather, earned, him a lot of money. The swish was a watered-down version of the bootleg, and it wasn't sold to his customers; he kept that for himself.

He started out drinking swish on the nights he was on duty. He stopped into The Dump two or three times a shift while driving up and down the highway, to check the crowd, as he told Ruby, but it was really to suck a few back. He did that for a long while, until, one night there was a three—car pile-up down the highway, and another district officer showed up at the crash site while Judd was working it. It didn't take the other officer long to figure out that Judd was working while tanked on moonshine whiskey. Ruby still hadn't the foggiest notion how he'd saved his job, but it was sometime after that night that the swish-barrel showed up.

Now, whenever Judd came into The Dump while on the clock, Wally McDonald in tow, Ruby served him swish. Wally, not being an officer of the law, drank the high-octane version, and/or beer (mostly and), and rode shotgun three sheets to the wind.

No one, not even Wally, knew about the swish-barrel. Judd was a proud man, and most proud of the idea that he could drink any other man under the table, even if he had to cheat to do it. It wasn't long before he was drinking swish on the nights that he didn't have to work, as well, because he'd figured out a way to make even more money out of his clientele.

He invented a drinking game. The rules were simple. If you wanted in, you bought a shot, and threw a dollar into the pot. You drank your shot. Then you bought another shot, and threw another dollar into the pot - several more times. If you were still standing, and hadn't puked yet or run out of money, you bought another shot. Sometimes you played against Judd, and sometimes you played against Judd as well as everybody else in The Dump. Judd was always the last man standing, and so he always won the take. He made money hand over fist; nobody got in the game without a dollar for the pot, and Judd didn't let anybody run a tab.

Ruby figured that the only reason the idiots kept playing was that they were generally too drunk to realize that Judd was sober. Every night they played, they were certain that someone would topple the champ. And every night they played, Ruby spent the majority of her shift mopping up vomit, while Judd crowed over his winnings.

Wally never played the whiskey game, not having any money of his own, but sometimes The Little Drunk would throw a dollar or two in. Ruby couldn't decide if she preferred The Little Drunk playing the whiskey game or not; when he played, he went up to his room sooner, and so got out from under her feet, but that meant that he lay in a wet straw tick longer. She couldn't change it with him in it, and it had got so that she couldn't quite get that room to let go the smell of stale urine anymore.

A lot of the time, too, when The Little Drunk played the whiskey game, he passed out in the bar, which meant Ruby had to drag him up the stairs at the end of her shift. It was on one of those nights that she finally hit her limit - again - and gave Judd Gulley what-for. This time, she did it in front of his customers, and she regretted it almost instantly.

It had looked, at first, as if it would be an easy Saturday night, as far as Saturday nights at The Dump went. There weren't many regulars there at all; there was a charity Donkey Baseball game scheduled for the next afternoon, and a lot of the fellows who would normally be at The Dump on a Saturday night were playing ball in that game, so Ruby figured they were all home in bed at that hour.

It was close to 1 am, and Judd was off that night, so he'd been in the bar since before it opened, swigging back swish, and bemoaning the small crowd; all of them were drinking slow tonight. Church in the morning, and the thought of Donkey Baseball kept them from carousing much - nobody wanted to endure a hangover and a pack of obstinate donkeys.

It didn't surprise Ruby at all when Judd stood up and called out, "Howsabout a game of whiskey, boys?" to the few that were present. Nor did it surprise her when they all jumped at the chance to see the champ whipped, finally. After all, Judd appeared to be more in his cups than the rest of them combined. Even The Little Drunk bought in.

The game was going for an hour when the first man fell. Before he fell, though, he upchucked, right on the table. His timing couldn't have been worse. Ruby had just set down a plate of hash and runny eggs in front of Wally, who wasn't altogether too tight, as of yet, but the smell of his supper, coupled with the sound of the loser retching, and followed by the sight of a half-digested meal landing next to Wally's own plate, was all it took for Wally to bring up what was left of his lunch - all over The Little Drunk, who had quietly fallen asleep in the chair beside him.

Ruby hit the roof.

"Judd Gulley, you have ticked me off for the last time!" she hollered, but even as she yelled at him, she was starting to clean up the mess. She got a pail from behind the bar and began to scrape the mess off the table and into it.

Judd, along with every man in the bar, even Wally, having proven that the saying "better out than in" must hold true, began to laugh riotously. Ruby slapped Wally with the dishrag.

"You oughtta be ashamed of yourself! Look at this mess! And if you think I'm gonna put Wilson to bed in that condition, Judd, you have yourself another think coming! I have had enough! I quit! I won't put up with this business one more minute!"

 All Ruby wanted to do was stomp out the door,

but for some reason that belied her own words, she continued to clean the table as she quit her job.

"Now, Ruby…." Judd laughed, in a cajoling voice, as he went behind the bar, himself. "You know we're just playing."

"Just playing, my patoot!" Ruby yelled back, beginning to mop the puke off The Little Drunk's shirt. "You get that drunk outta here!" She pointed at the passed-out loser of the game.

"In fact, all of you just get the hell out! This is the last time I clean up a mess like this! Go!" She hadn't noticed Judd coming back from behind the bar, handcuffs in hand, until it was too late. Before she knew it, Judd had placed one cuff around the skinny wrist of The Little Drunk, and the other around one of Ruby's own. She was surprised into silence.

Judd laughed long and hard, along with the rest of them. "Why, Ruby, you can't quit! How would I ever get along without you? Here's a little bonus for you," he said, as he swept the money pot from the center of the table, and tucked the bills into Ruby's apron. "I'm gonna take Reg home, now. Let's go, boys. Let's just close up early, and give Ruby a chance to cool off and clean up some. She's had herself a rough shift."

And with that, Judd and Wally hiked Reg up off the floor and half-walked, half-dragged him out the door, the rest of "the boys" trailing behind, leaving Ruby stunned, and hand-cuffed to The Little Drunk, who slept in his chair, oblivious.

PART III: THE HANDCUFFS

"Well, now. Ain't this just a fine mess?" Ruby slapped The Little Drunk on the shoulder with her free hand. "Wilson! Hey!"

The Little Drunk stirred in his chair slightly and mumbled something.

"What's that…?" asked Ruby.

"You can't fill the holes in my bowling ball," he said. Well, that's what Ruby thought he might have said, but the truth was, she had trouble carrying on a conversation with Wilson Jones on a good day. This was most certainly not a good day.

"Wilson, I swear you are not quite right in the head. Wake up, now. I have to get this place cleaned up, and I don't know how I'm gonna manage, hitched up to you like this. Wake up!"

She slapped him again, harder this time. The Little Drunk started awake.

"It was a fairy! It must have been!"

Ruby shook her head in disgust. "If you're friendly with fairies, Wilson Jones, I would surely appreciate you calling on one that can magic us out of these handcuffs."

Wilson looked at the handcuff on his wrist in surprise.

"Why, Ruby! What the heck sakes have we been getting up to?!"

"Nothing but being the butt of Judd Gulley's idiot wit, that's all, Wilson. Now get up off that chair and walk, would you? I can't drag you around the room and still clean it up, can I?"

The Little Drunk hauled himself up with Ruby's help. Ruby took him by the wrist and walked him back to the kitchen, carrying the bucket. Wilson was pretty much done in, having drunk too many shots of whiskey. Ruby wondered if he had more booze than blood anymore. She had to walk slowly enough for him to keep up, steadying him all the way to the back.

They went out the back door and across the far end of the parking lot to the edge of the tree-line, where Ruby emptied the pail. Damn stinking mess, she thought to herself, hauling The Little Drunk around again, and leading him back to the building.

She stoked the fire in the old cook stove, swearing under her breath at Judd's stinginess. He kept the cook stove for Ruby to cook the meals of his customers on, rather than purchase a propane or electric stove. The cook stove had a water reservoir, and so as long as she kept it full of water, and wood on the fire, she had plenty of hot water for cleaning and dishes. As far as Judd was concerned, that was good enough for The Dump, and so he'd never bothered to hook up a hot water line to the kitchen sink. The only concession he'd made for hot running water led to the shower stall upstairs, and he complained about that every time he got the hydro bill in the mail.

Ruby ladled hot water from the reservoir into the pail, sloshed it around, and emptied it out the back door. She rinsed the pail a second time, the whole procedure taking three times as long as it would have if she weren't handcuffed to The Little Drunk.

Every time she tried to use her right hand, Wilson's own would dangle along like a dead thing, getting in the way. What made matters even more inconvenient, was that Judd had cuffed both their right hands together, so Wilson had to stand directly behind her in order to be out of the way. Poor Wilson didn't like the situation any better than Ruby, and unless she warned him she was about to move that arm, he would automatically try to pull his own back. Every now and again, he would say something bizarre or cryptic.

Ruby set about cleaning The Dump, all the while wondering how long Judd intended to leave them cuffed together. She worried that he wouldn't bother to come back for hours, and could just picture him and Wally McDonald rolling in laughter over the prank.

Meantime, much as she would have liked to leave the clean-up for after she was freed, she knew it would only take that much longer to do if the food dried on the plates and the tables sat sticky overnight. Already, she had forgot she'd "quit" the job.

First things first; she hauled all the dirty dishes and whiskey glasses to the kitchen and scraped the plates into Judd's dog-pail. The stingy bastard, true to form, fed his dog bar scraps.

Normally, clearing the tables at the end of the night, and setting the dishes to soak while she scrubbed at the booze rings and cigarette burns on the tables would have taken about twenty minutes. Cuffed to The Little Drunk, especially in such a cross-wise manner, it took Ruby almost two hours, with still no sign of Judd returning. She'd swear he'd done it just that way to make the situation even worse for her.

Wilson tried to do his part by surreptitiously downing any liquid remaining in the bottoms of glasses and beer bottles. When Ruby caught him at it, she bawled him out. The last thing she needed was The Little Drunk passing out again.

"How many thumbs do you need?" Wilson asked, after she'd told him off for the third time.

By the time she was ready to do the dishes, she realized the impossibility of doing so. She pictured what might happen if she repeatedly dunked The Little Drunk's hand into a sink full of hot water. She also pictured accidentally injuring him with a sharp knife or a broken bar glass. Truth be told, she had mean, dark thoughts of injuring him on purpose, just because he was slowing her down. Perhaps there was more of her mother in Ruby than she'd like to admit.

It was 3:30 in the morning. Ruby had no idea if Judd planned on returning or not. She wouldn't put it past him to pretend to forget all about the incident until Sunday afternoon, and then cackle over it. She realized the futility of attempting any more work, and sat down at a table to think things through.

"Wilson, do you have any cigarettes?" Ruby didn't generally smoke, but she indulged now and again, especially when she was upset. She had smoked more often in the past two years, since working at The Dump than during all the years since she had taken that first puff at sixteen years old.

She grimaced as Wilson dug into his pants pocket, her own hand dragging across his leg in the process. He came up with a much-creased, dirty package of loose tobacco. Well, hell. Ruby didn't exactly cherish the idea of trying to smoke a badly put together roll-your-own cigarette - how tightly could a vellum paper be rolled when the hand doing the rolling was handcuffed to somebody else's arm, after all?

The Little Drunk astounded her by deftly rolling a perfect cigarette, using only his left hand. He handed it to her, and just as quickly rolled a second. Then he surprised her again by proffering the flame from a beautifully engraved silver-plated lighter.

"Why, Wilson! That's a lovely piece of work, now, ain't it? Where did you ever come to own such a thing?"

The Little Drunk smiled and blushed. "A girl gave me that," he said.

Ruby didn't know whether to be more surprised that a girl had ever looked twice at Wilson Jones, or that he'd opened his mouth and out came a string of sensible words. Then she remembered what time it was, and tried to figure a way out of the mess she was in. She was worn out, and just wanted to go home.

She smoked her cigarette, and contemplated the reaction from her mother in the morning, if Ruby came to the breakfast table handcuffed to Wilson Jones. She shuddered at the thought. Then it occurred to her that if there was to be any sleep to be had at all that night, she had to find a way out of the cuffs – she had no intention of sharing sleeping accommodations, no matter how innocently, with Wilson Jones, who hadn't made it through a single weekend these last two years without wetting the bed.

She took a closer look at the silver bracelet encircling her wrist. Could she pick it? She had no idea. How easy might it be to pick a standard set of police handcuffs? Never mind that Ruby had never attempted to pick a lock in her life. She had to try now, though; she couldn't sit up all night. She was half-asleep already, and The Little Drunk had dozed off in his chair while she ruminated.

She dug a bobby pin out of her hair, bent it reasonably straight, and scraped the plastic coating off one end with her teeth. She attempted to stick the flat end of the pin into the tiny keyhole on the handcuff and missed, swearing under her breath. She was right-handed, and that was the hand in the cuff.

When she finally did manage to get the end of the bobby pin into the keyhole, her stupid hand wouldn't cooperate when she tried to twist it. If she tried to twist clockwise, her hand seemed to be attempting to move the pin counter-clockwise. She threw the bobby pin down on the table, annoyed.

Ruby wondered if she could somehow cut through the chain between the cuffs, and envisioned the little slaughter axe her mother used to kill the chickens. That may very well work, for all she knew, if someone else were wielding it. She wouldn't dare attempt a hard chop using her left hand; she'd likely miss, and cut her good hand off at the wrist. She shuddered at the thought of trusting Wilson Jones with even a butter knife, never mind letting him aim an axe anywhere that close to her. He may be a good logger when he was sober, but she had no intention of letting him show off his prowess tonight, while this deep in his cups.

She finally conceded that unless Judd Gulley waltzed back into The Dump, and in short order, she would have to sleep on a damp and pissy-smelling dirty straw tick – handcuffed to Wilson

Jones. In her wildest of imaginations, she never could have pictured such a thing. Imagination, truthfully, had never been one of Ruby's stronger points.

She shook The Little Drunk awake, and stood him on his feet.

"Come on, Wilson. We're going upstairs."

She led him first out the back door again, though, to the edge of the parking lot. Judd, not surprisingly, had no indoor toilet facilities at The Dump. Instead, he had built a ramshackle outhouse for the comfort of his clientele, which Ruby, truthfully, didn't really mind using unless it was wintertime. A well-maintained outhouse didn't stink, and Ruby knew how to maintain one properly.

Most of the men could only be bothered to use the outhouse for "certain" ablutions, mind you; for more frequent duties, they had got into the habit of standing along the line of rocks at the back end of the parking lot and just aiming at the bushes. You could see the "unofficial" bathroom facilities marked with a line of withered, dead foliage a foot or so beyond the rocks.

This is where Ruby led The Little Drunk, and ordered him to "do his business", while she turned her back. This made it difficult for Wilson, as his own arm ended up bent behind his back, causing him to weave unsteadily. There was nothing for it, though, but to try to brace him enough so as not to tip himself over; Ruby had no intention of waking up in a wet straw tick, in the morning.

Wilson's duty done and over, she half-walked, half-carried him up the stairs and into his room. She sat him down on the bed while she pulled off his boots; a difficult procedure, since he had to bend double to accommodate the effort, cuffed together such as they were. While pulling off the second boot, Ruby heard a long, wet burp escape The Little Drunk.

"Wilson Jones, don't you dare barf on me," she snapped. "I've had enough of that business today!" She yanked hard on the boot, and when it let go his foot, she sat back on the floor with a thump. Wilson was yanked straight off the bed face-first onto the floor. *Good Christ, I hope I didn't just give his brains an extra scramble…* Ruby thought to herself, but when she took a hard look at him, he didn't seem any more damaged than usual.

She shut the light and got him onto the bed, and reluctantly lay down beside him, her right arm crossed over her body. What a nasty place to sleep! In the morning, she was going to hunt down Judd Gulley and give him what-for. Then she would never set foot in The Dump again.

Just before she drifted off, she nudged The Little Drunk.

"If you wet this bed tonight, Wilson Jones, I will throttle you," she said.

"Pickles," Wilson mumbled. "Good eatin'."

PART IV: THE GREAT ESCAPE

Ruby was having a lovely dream. She knew it was a dream because she could hear Roy snoring, but Roy was dead two years last Christmas. She dreamed she lay in bed in the early morning; the birds were singing to beat the band, and she knew it would be a stunningly bright summer day by the way the light filtered in through her eyelids.

Her youngest, Mary, was snuggled up in front of her, having crawled into bed with them some time through the night, like she'd done when she was a wee sma'. Ruby held her close and squeezed her a little tighter. In her dream, it became Mary that was snoring like a saw, and Ruby started to giggle. Then the smell hit her.

Her eyes flew open, and she was staring down at

the top of The Little Drunk's greasy head. He stunk of piss and vomit, and last night's liquor. When she realized she was wet from the waist down, Ruby's stomach did a slow roll. Here she was, arms wrapped around Wilson Jones, handcuffed to him, even, and he'd gone and wet the bed sometime before she'd woken up. Her dream shattered to bits, she was livid.

"Wilson, you little drunk, I could throttle you!" she hollered at him. He jumped to his feet, fully awake and scared to death. Ruby was hauled across the bed by the handcuff. Awareness slowly dawned on The Little Drunk's face, and he stood there, chin down, looking ashamed of himself.

"Good Christ, Wilson, if you can't control yourself, you oughtta not drink!" Ruby yelled again, not in the least bit sorry for shouting at him. She untangled herself, and stood up. She was soaked through her clothes from the bodice of her dress down to the hem, and ready to spit.

Worse, she'd forgotten to take her apron off, and the bundle of paper money Judd had stuffed in her pocket was scattered all over the wet tick, stuck to the covers that she hadn't bothered to turn down when they'd gone to sleep. When she saw Judd Gulley she would give him a dressing-down like he'd never had before.

Thinking of Judd, Ruby hoped he'd returned to The Dump, and was waiting downstairs in the bar. She'd put up with his mouth just long enough to get the cuffs off, and then she'd tell him where he could stick his job. If he tried to give her more money, she'd dang well take every cent, and then tell him to stick the job even farther. She'd had her limit, she had. Judd Gulley could wash his own sheets and blankets.

She propelled Wilson down the stairs, but of course, there was no Judd Gulley to be seen. That was alright with Ruby; she knew where he lived, and she intended to give him a rude awakening.

The state that both she and The Little Drunk were in, though, gave her pause for thought. She didn't want to stink up her truck. How was she ever going to manage to get the two of them cleaned up? She was mad enough, that if there had been a hose outside, she would've just hosed Wilson down in icy water, but there was no such thing as a garden hose at The Dump. They would have to use the shower upstairs.

She sighed and hauled Wilson back up the stairs. She took her apron off and turned on the shower, shoving The Little Drunk into the stall, clothes and all. She handed him a bar of soap and instructed him to start scrubbing, beginning with his shirt, which was still covered with Wally McDonald's dried puke.

She wondered if Wilson ever bothered to shower often enough to know how to go about it properly; she had to give him new instructions every few minutes. She finally finished the job herself, since her entire right arm had to be in the shower with him anyway.

When she thought he was clean enough to do, she spread a towel on the floor and had him stand on it while she squeezed water out of his clothes as best she could. Then she stepped under the water herself. Of course, it wasn't hot anymore, and by the time she'd scrubbed herself and her dress down, it was freezing. At least she didn't stink as bad, but she expected she'd be uncomfortable wearing wet clothing for the next hour or two.

She crossed to Wilson's room, hauling him along,

and peeled the money off the bed. Holding the bills gingerly by the corners, she led Wilson back down the stairs to the kitchen. The fire in the cook stove had gone out long ago, but the water in the reservoir was still uncomfortably hot to touch. She put the money in a pan and poured water over it.

She thought she really ought to feed Wilson some breakfast, but the idea of trying to get a fire going in the old stove with him cuffed to her arm tired her out before she'd fully formed it in her mind. Breakfast for the both of them would have to wait until Judd got these cuffs off. She thought of the large breakfast her mother would be serving about now, and her stomach growled.

Her mother! Good Lord, she hadn't let her mother know she wasn't coming home. There was no phone at The Dump, of course; she'd have to remember to stop at the highway corner before she turned off the side road, and use the pay phone. She had no idea what she would say, but she'd have to come up with something. She'd need an excuse for missing church, but if being handcuffed to Wilson Jones overnight wasn't reason enough to miss church, she guessed she'd just burn in hell.

"Come on, Wilson. Let's go find Judd and Wally. I have some yelling to do."

It wasn't until they got into the cab of Ruby's old Ford that she realized their problems were just beginning. She couldn't shift gears unless The Little Drunk was sitting smack up against her. There was no way to avoid driving straight down Main Street to get to Judd's house.

Everybody and his brother and his cousin's Aunt Grace would be on their way to church, and here she would be, driving up the main drag for all to see, with Wilson Jones practically sitting in her lap. The only people that rode around like that were the teeny-boppers, and even they had the sense not to be so indiscreet on a Sunday morning. This may have been the first time in all her 30-something years that Ruby truly felt that life just wasn't fair.

She remembered in the nick of time to stop at the pay phone, and then had to go through more rigamarole to make the call. First of all, she had no change, and had to ask Wilson to dig through his pockets. Then she had to pick through the mess of screws and coins he came up with to find a nickel.

She lifted the receiver. There was a buzz-click sound and then the operator came on the line.

"Operator…"

"Hey, Flora; it's Ruby Daniel. Will you ring home for me, please?"

"Well, hey there, Ruby, sure thing. Two longs and a short?"

"That's right."

There was another buzz-click followed by a pause. Sometimes when placing a call, you could hear the ghost of a ring from far, far away. Most times, you heard nothing but a hum, which let you know the operator was still on the line. Today it was just the hum, but Ruby knew the phone in the front hallway at home was sounding out two long buzzing rings followed by a short, sharp one, over and over.

Ruby grimaced a little, knowing that the same ring – her ring – was blasting in every other house up the North Side Road, and hoped the neighbours were too busy with church preparations to sneakily pick up their receivers once the ringing stopped. She pictured her mother lumbering up the hall toward the phone, muttering for the caller to wait for her, she was a-coming.

"HULLO! DANIEL!!" Her mother always hollered into the phone, certain it was the only way to be heard at all.

"Ma?"

"RUBY, WHERE THE BEJEEZUS ARE YOU AT?! WE'RE GONNA BE LATE FOR SERVICE! THE KIDS IS ALREADY DRESSED!"

"I run into a spot at The Dump, Ma. Listen -"

"WHAT HAPPENED?"

Ruby could still hear the tell-tale hum that indicated Flora was listening in on the call. There was no way on God's green earth she was going to tell her mother what happened.

"Nothing serious, Ma, but listen, I can't get home in time for church. You gotta ask up the line for a lift in. I'll do my best to get there before it's over." She knew there was no way she would ever make that service, but hopefully that would be enough explanation for her mother.

"Y'ALRIGHT?"

Just then, Ruby heard a muffled ringing noise, and knew Flora had to direct a call from another party line. There was that buzz-click again, and then the hum disappeared. Still, Ruby wasn't taking any chances.

"Yeah, Ma; I'm fine and all. I'll see you at church."

She hung up the phone and waited for Flora to ring back. Her right arm was feeling almost dead, as she'd had to have it hanging through the door of the truck this whole time. When the phone buzzed, she picked it up.

"Hey, Flora."

"Hey, Ruby. Five cents, please." Ruby dropped her nickel in the slot, and listened to it tumble down into the bowels of the pay phone. Flora thanked her kindly, and rang off. Ruby got back in the truck, praying that she wouldn't run into the whole town on Main Street. She shook the tingles out of her arm before she turned the ignition, making The Little Drunk laugh. Ruby couldn't wait to get to Judd's house.

Highway 17 ran smack through the middle of

town, so, for a short stretch, the highway actually became Main Street. A quarter of a mile from The Dump Side Road, the highway curved left through a rock cut, and suddenly you were among storefronts and pedestrians.

This left Ruby precious little time to decide what to do about gossipy church-goers who might notice Wilson Jones and Ruby Daniel practically spooning in the cab of her truck, at 10 am on a Sunday morning. They'd have a hay day, she knew, and she'd be a long time living it down. In fact, she figured people would bring it up and laugh every now and again for years after she was in the ground.

The truck was just going into the curve when Ruby had an idea.

"Wilson, get on the floor," she ordered, and shoved him off the seat. He lay on the floor under the dashboard with his right arm hovering between the seat and the stick, hanging off Ruby's arm, as her hand rested on the gear-shift. She shifted down to first as they came out of the curve and onto Main Street, and The Little Drunk yelped as his arm was yanked around.

Sure enough, the church parking lot was full, and

cars were lined up along the sidewalk in front. The town was tiny, but people came in from all over the outlying district for church on Sundays. The only time Main Street was as busy as on a Sunday morning was during the Community Day parade.

She drove down Main Street, nodding at folks that waved, and reminding herself over and over that the only reason they were staring at her was that she was driving right past the church instead of parking and walking inside with the rest of them. She was relieved to finally turn down Judd's Street.

She parked in front of Judd's house. His cruiser wasn't in the drive. Ruby sat dejected, wondering what to do next. Wilson started to climb back up on the seat and she shoved him back down, a little absently.

She remembered that Wally McDonald had a cousin in the next town up the line, and wondered at the chances that they might be there. She checked her gas gauge and wondered if she had enough fuel to get there and back. Maybe she could fill up at Bernie's station on the way out of town; he'd be at church anyhow.

She drove back to Main Street and turned right.

Looking left, she could see the street was still filled with cars, but there were no signs of people, so service must have started. She felt better about that, as she pulled into Bernie's and dragged The Little Drunk out of the truck. She pumped the tank full, and went into the building to leave Bernie a note, saying she'd be by to pay him the next day.

By the time she got to Wally's cousin's place, Wilson was asleep with his head on her shoulder. No Judd. No Wally. No cruiser. She decided to drive the side roads, hoping to catch sight of Judd's car somewhere.

Two and a half hours later they were still driving around, and she was no closer to getting out of this mess than she had been when she woke up that morning. She shoved The Little Drunk back down on the floor while she drove through town again. The streets were deserted, which was not unusual for a Sunday afternoon, really, but it was awful strange that there weren't vehicles in the driveways at least. Ruby was starting to feel like she was starring in one of the popular horror movies the kids watched at the theatre in the next town over on

Saturday nights.

She was out of ideas. She drove back to The Dump, wondering what the heck to do next. When she hustled Wilson through the door, she stopped short in surprise.

There was a rope strung across the room, and hanging from it were the sheets and blankets from The Little Drunk's bed, clean and drying. The now-empty straw tick was hanging there, too, and her apron was laid out to dry over the backs of a couple of chairs. The floor had been scrubbed. Sitting at the bar with a glass of whiskey in front of her, was Ruby's mother.

"Ruby, I got to tell you, you left this place a right mess. Shameful." She made a face into her whiskey glass. "Almost as shameful as this watery piss Judd Gulley tries to pass off as booze."

Ruby was having a hard time recovering from the shock of seeing her mother in such a place as The Dump, let alone drinking whiskey on a Sunday afternoon. She almost felt sorry for her, though; of all the barrels her mother could have chosen to draw from, she'd managed to pick the only one full of swish.

"I been looking for Judd. What are you doing here, Ma?"

"I come to see what the bejeezus was going on, didn't I? Why are you hog-tied to Wilson Jones of all people?"

"Fairies," Wilson said.

"Fairies, my patoot," snorted Ruby's mother. "Judd Gulley'll have some come-uppance out of this business, I guess. S'pose you clean forgot about the Donkey baseball match today. That's where he'll be, dollars to donuts." Her mother looked her up and down. "Just as well, by the look of you. Sit down, and let's get you fixed up."

Ruby and The Little Drunk sat down across from each other while Ruby's mother took a closer look at the handcuffs.

"Ain't gonna work, Ma," said Ruby as her mother picked up the straightened bobby pin that Ruby had dropped on the table in disgust the night before.

Three seconds later, her wrist was free of the cuff, and Wilson's followed suit shortly. His face split into a grin and he bobbed his head at Ruby's mother in thanks. Ruby just sat there, stunned, rubbing her wrist.

"Betcher hungry as a bear, ain't you, Wilson?" Ruby's mother patted him on the head and sat down, tucking the handcuffs into the pocket of her apron. "Ruby, go on in the kitchen and lift us all a bowl of stew. How's your sister keeping, Wilson?"

Ruby left them talking family, surprised that The Little Drunk managed to have a normal conversation with her mother. Most folks were a little frightened of the woman. And Ruby had a new respect for her. Where in the world did she learn to open a handcuff with a bobby pin?!

The kitchen was spotless. On the cook stove, a pot of beef stew was simmering nicely. As Ruby was ladling it into bowls, she noticed the money Judd had stuffed into her apron was all spread out, now dry on the warming shelf. She folded up the bills and tucked them away, smiling. Her mother had taken care of everything while Ruby was gallivanting all over the countryside in search of Judd.

She brought the stew out to the bar, and while they ate, Ruby thanked her mother for cleaning the place while she was gone. Ruby's mother said that was fine. Ruby said she was quitting Judd Gulley for good after this business. Her mother said she most certainly was not.

"You'll show for work just like you always do on Friday night."

"Not this time, Ma. I'm done."

"No, you ain't. And I'm not done with Judd Gulley, either. I have me a bit of an idea."

"Fairies," said Wilson, around a mouthful of beef stew.

PART V: REVENGE

Ruby's life went on pretty much the same after the handcuff incident. Ruby didn't like it much, but then, she hadn't liked it much before, either. And she'd learned enough shocking things about her mother over the past while, that she somehow trusted her to come up with the secret little plan for revenge against Judd Gulley. The more she thought about it, the more the idea of revenge struck Ruby as not only fair and just, but somehow an obligation. It was the waiting that was getting to her.

Judd spent a few weeks transparently not mentioning the handcuff incident at all. Every Friday night when Ruby came home, her mother would be at the kitchen table, working the crossword out of the paper, waiting for her. The first thing she would ask was whether or not Judd had mentioned "it" to Ruby, and every week, the answer was "No." This invariably sent her mother into gales of laughter. Finally, Ruby, in a fit of annoyance, asked why that was so funny.

"Oh, Ruby," her mother laughed, wiping her eyes on her apron. "Don't you see? It's driving him nuts! He can't figure out how you got out of that mess, and worse, he didn't get the laugh out of it that he was hopin' for. Nobody saw you handcuffed to Wilson Jones; even the fools that were there were too tight to remember it. There goes all Judd Gulley's fun, poor stupid sap." And off she went into another fit of laughter. Ruby remained unimpressed.

"Well, when are you gonna tell me this dastardly plan of yours? I'm not gonna keep going back into The Dump every weekend. You said you were gonna fix things, and here I am still schlomping booze to a bunch of drunks. I've had enough, Ma."

"Don't you worry none, Ruby. It won't be long now. Just let things get back to normal."

It wasn't until the following October, though, that Ruby finally had the chance to exact her revenge completely. Meanwhile, she spent the rest of the summer's weekends mopping spilled beer and puke, and changing the straw in The Little Drunk's tick. Wilson was a little more careful with the drink, now, though. He seemed to make slightly more sense when he was sober, she noticed, but he never missed a night of his bed-wetting routine.

Over the next little while, Judd slowly stopped looking at Ruby sideways, and got back into his routine of bellyaching, blustering and drinking his customers under the table while pocketing their hard-earned money, all the while cheating under their noses.

When the Whiskey Game had gone through several more weekends, Ruby's mother allowed the first step of her plan to be implemented. That first step alone seemed to take forever, because, as Ruby's mother said, it had to be done in stages for it to work. Judd may be a stupid galoot, but he knew his whiskey, and the change had to take place gradually.

On the last weekend in August, Ruby started to

"un-swish" the swish barrel.

The way Judd made his swish was to siphon half the whiskey out of a full barrel of straight stuff into a second barrel, and top that up with plain water. Then, every now and again, the barrel would be shaken around to even out the mix. Of course, this job, too, had fallen to Ruby, along with the rest of the grunt work involved with running The Dump.

Every time Ruby went into the stock room behind the bar, she would grab the barrel by the edges and give it a "swish". This did keep the mix even for the most part, but for good measure, Judd had her add a dipper or two of water now and again as the contents got close to the quarter mark. Ruby wondered if he was drinking whiskey-flavoured water by the time the swish hit the dregs.

"Prob'ly is," her mother stated flatly, when Ruby remarked on this.

"There's another good reason right there to take it slow. Just edge it up a quart at first and see if he notices."

He didn't. He started a game of Whiskey that very night, and Ruby held her breath while she watched him throw back his shot of swish, while the rest drank straight-up booze. Her heart gave a queer little flip-flop when a grimace came over Judd's face after he'd tossed the first shot or two back, but then she recognized it as what passed for his "fake face". If the other guys coughed and made a face, Judd felt he'd better, too, so as not to give away his game. Ruby shook her head, feeling somehow that it made the whole charade even more of a cheat than watering down his own whiskey just to win a stupid drinking game.

The very next night, she topped up the swish barrel with another quart of straight whiskey. She almost blew the whole plan right there, because Judd *did* notice this time. Luckily, it didn't occur to him that Ruby was up to any shenanigans; just that she might be off her game.

"You ain't been swishing that barrel," he hissed at her in the kitchen, after excusing himself for a "call of nature, boys!" Ruby thought fast and blasted him.

"Do you see that crowd out there?! Go swish your own barrel, Judd Gulley; I'm busy!" she hissed right back, and it seemed to mollify him. She did notice, later, that when he went in to swish the barrel, he also added three dippers full of water to it. Irritated, Ruby harrumphed to herself that it only saved her the bother of fixing her own mistake, anyway.

The following weekend, Ruby only added a half-quart of whiskey to the barrel on Friday night, and the second half-quart waited until Saturday night. She made sure to swish the barrel several times throughout the weekend, and Judd seemed none the wiser. He kept on winning the pot, too, so she figured she had a ways yet to go.

It wasn't until a Friday afternoon several weeks later that she came up against a flaw in her mother's plan. She drove to the phone booth in a panic and called home.

"HULLO! DANIEL!!" yelled her mother after thirteen rings.

"I got a problem, Ma," Ruby began.

"Y'ALRIGHT?"

"Yeah, but the barrel's empty and Judd's already

made his mix."

"SO? START OVER."

"What do you mean, 'start over'?! I got no idea where we're at!"

"GOOD CHRIST, I'VE RAISED AN IJIT. COME GET ME; I'LL DO IT MYSELF."

So, Ruby went and picked her mother up and brought her back to The Dump, where she asked Ruby question after question. How full was the barrel when she'd added that first quart of whiskey? How many quarts had she added since? How often did Judd go in there and add water to the mix, and how much did he add? Ruby answered all these questions while her mother worked out figures on a notepad, licking the stub of an old pencil between chicken scratches.

"Don't we need to know how many quarts fit in a barrel?" Ruby finally asked.

"I know how many quarts fit in a whiskey barrel," her mother replied, and Ruby believed her. Ruby would believe the sky was green if her mother said it, now.

After a time, Ruby's mother told her how much swish she needed to siphon from the barrel and replace with straight whiskey. Ruby didn't question her; she went straight to work. And sure enough, Judd didn't blink once that night, but for the first time, Ruby noticed he seemed just a little wobbly on his feet. She began to feel, finally, that her mother's idea might really work.

She wasn't pleased for long, however. That night, Wally and several others totaled the place with a knock-down, drag-out fist fight, overturning tables and breaking chairs. The finale came when each and all got sick in a different corner and Judd gave them the toss. He even banished Wally, sending him out to sleep it off in the back of the cruiser. As Ruby sighed and began to set the place to rights again, she caught The Little Drunk's eye. He gave her a sly wink.

"Fish always stinks from the head downwards," he intoned soberly.

"I don't know what that means, Wilson, but I'm sure you're right," Ruby replied. Wilson grinned at her, and then got up and helped her move the furniture back where it belonged.

It was half-way through October when her mother told her to back off with the whiskey.

"Just let it ride as it is, Ruby; we don't want him losin' that game for two more Fridays."

Ruby was mad. "What? Why not, Ma?! I been a long time waiting already, and I want outta there!"

Ruby's mother wouldn't budge, though. Ruby had to try to keep the swish barrel at the same strength for the next two weeks – no easy feat without her mother there to work the figures, but she managed. On the last Friday of October, her mother gave Ruby new instructions as they were tidying up the breakfast dishes.

"Tonight, bump it up a little."

Vexed, Ruby asked, "Ma, when's this gonna be done and over with?"

Her mother laughed, "This is it, Ruby. Tonight Judd Gulley gets his comeuppance. Well, I guess that'll come tomorrow, but it starts tonight, don't it?"

"What do you mean, tomorrow? This is it. I'm not

going back in that place again after tonight!"

"Nor will you need to, Ruby," her mother tried to soothe her. "And the very second you see Judd start to wobble tonight, I want you to start serving him straight shots."

Ruby went in to The Dump that afternoon in a fair state of mind, looking forward to finally being free of the place. Her good mood was dampened a little when she found Judd already there, and in one foul temper, to boot. She made herself scarce in the kitchen, peeling potatoes for the supper hour, rather than deal with him.

As the evening wore on, she began to get nervous. Judd was off-duty, and so he started drinking early. She was so nervous about what was about to come that she nearly forgot to "bump up" the swish barrel as per her mother's instructions. By the time she remembered, the place was full and she didn't have time to go back and do it. It was Judd, himself, that fixed that problem for her.

"Go swish that barrel, would you?" he demanded in her ear, as she scrubbed down a table.

"My, but aren't you the ornery one, tonight, Judd

Gulley," she snarled at him, but she went readily enough, and she did swish the barrel – but only after she'd topped it up with a full quart of straight whiskey. Her hand shook a little when she set down the first of those stronger shots in front of Judd. She was sure he would notice this time, but her mother was right after all.

After being slowly coaxed back onto the real thing, or, at least, a stronger-than-usual version of it, Judd had lost the ability to taste the difference. He'd also lost what little skill he'd had in holding his liquor; he was showing signs of drunkenness before he called the first game of Whiskey, and had even let Wally McDonald in on the game for once.

The first man out was The Little Drunk, and Ruby helped him up the stairs and into bed. She didn't have the heart to warn him not to wet his bed, as usual, knowing what was coming.

Three shots into the next game, Judd began to weave a little as he set his glass down on the table. Ruby poured the next round, and this time all the shots on the tray were the real deal. She held her breath as Judd downed his, but he didn't seem to know the difference. That was the round that Wally passed out on, before he'd even lifted his glass.

"Hey!" Judd yelled at him. "Wake up, you drunk arse, you! We're in the middle of a game, here!"

When Wally didn't twitch, Judd picked up the shot glass and threw it back himself.

"No refunds, either. That'll teach you," which was as strange thing to say, considering he'd been paying for Wally's shots. He was having trouble speaking now, but didn't seem to notice.

The rest of the fellas at the table did, though. Slowly, a new light seemed to seep into their eyes, as they began to hope that this might be the night that the King of Whiskey was finally toppled.

They quickly threw another dollar each into the center of the table, and urged Ruby to bring on another tray of shots. That round went by with all players still in, although Judd seemed to lean further and further to the left.

The next round was the end for one more, but it wasn't Judd. Ruby was relieved that so far, none had upchucked, but she didn't hold out much hope for things to remain that way. Judd was three sheets to the wind, but he still didn't seem to be close to losing the game.

There were three left in, aside from him, and one player wanted to stand down. Judd berated him, until he agreed to go one more round… and that's when everything went to hell.

The money was thrown in the pot. The whiskey was poured, and the shots were thrown back. Judd had a bit of a time with his. He gurgled. He swallowed hard. He wove back and forth in his chair. Everybody at the table, and Ruby from the bar, watched intently, waiting to see if he would fall over, retch, or both. He did neither.

Judd's gaze roamed drunkenly over the room and slowly settled on Ruby. He blinked a few times, trying to focus on her face.

"You," he slurred, "You switched barrels on me."

Ruby's hands shook as she wiped down the bar, but she stared him down.

The rest of the boys looked from Ruby to Judd and back again. Finally one of them spoke up.

"What's he talking about, Ruby?"

"I'm sure I've no idea, Doug," Ruby replied.

"Oh, yes, you do, you ol' prude, you!" roared Judd. He stood up suddenly, and just as suddenly sat right back down again.

"You been cheating us all along, ain't you Judd?" Doug accused him. The rest looked too shocked to speak, but the truth was slowly dawning on them.

"Now, Doug…" Judd began. And then he lay his head down on the table, belched once, and started to snore.

"Why, that bastard!" yelled Doug. "I've a mind to-"

"Sit down, Doug Ennis. You're not gonna do a thing but get yourself and your pals home." It was Ruby's mother, standing in the doorway. "You might just divvy up that pot on the table, 'fore you leave. Go on now. Bar's closing."

Ruby had no idea why her mother had cut it so close, unless she'd sat in the parking lot a spell, but she was relieved to see her, just the same. She took the bag of clothes that her mother handed her and went upstairs with them.

As the last of the clientele vacated the premises,

Ruby gently woke the Little Drunk. He was a mess, having already wet his bed, but this time, Ruby didn't yell at him. This time she was pleased.

"Come on, Wilson, get up. I've got some clean clothes here for you, but you gotta change downstairs. Can you manage to get down there do you think?"

"If there's turnips, I'll manage."

"That almost makes some sense, Wilson. Maybe I'll cook you up some at my place. You're gonna sleep there tonight."

Wilson managed the stairs nicely, with a little help, and bobbed his head at Ruby's mother.

"Set yourself down, Wilson. We'll just be a little bit longer," she said. "Grab an arm, Ruby."

Ruby took hold of Judd and helped her mother drag him up the stairs. He was a heavy man, and a dead weight. By the time they'd dumped him on the wet straw tick, they were both fairly out of puff.

"One more, Ruby. Let's get 'er done," said her mother. Ruby didn't think she could pull another drunk up those stairs, but Wally helped himself some, although he didn't seem to have his eyes open. When they lay him down next to Judd, he cuddled right up to him. Ruby's mother snorted.

"Well, wouldja look at that?" she said. "Snug as two bugs in a rug. You bring those cuffs, Ruby?"

Ruby pulled Judd's handcuffs from her apron pocket. She never could understand why he hadn't demanded them back, but her mother maintained it was because he was too embarrassed to, seeing as his joke on her hadn't panned out the way he'd intended.

"Just leave them on the bed table, there. Go on down and make sure that Little Drunk ain't asleep, and I'll be right along."

"What are you going to do, Ma?"

"Never you mind, Ruby. I'll be right down."

And she was too, in short order, with her arms full of Judd and Wally's clothes.

"What?" she said, at Ruby's look. "You don't think they deserve it?"

Ruby laughed. Yes, she thought. They sure do deserve it.

Wilson had fallen asleep after all, with his head on the bar, and it took some doing to wake him up. Ruby's mother had to offer him a full-on farmer's breakfast once they got home in order convince him that he'd be best off to spend the rest of the night at the chicken farm.

With the prospect of scrambled eggs, sausage, fried potatoes, and fresh hot-buttered biscuits in his very near future, Wilson rallied himself off his stool and toward the door, looking fairly near-sober.

When they got outside, Ruby was confused.

"Where's the truck?" she demanded of her mother.

"I had Junior Briggs from up the line drop me off and bring his boy with him. The boy took your truck up and left it at the phone booth for us."

"But why would you do that, for God's sake?!"

"Why, we'll just drive Judd's cruiser on up and leave it for him to find in the morning, why not?" said her mother, opening the back door of the car, and tossing in the bundle of Judd and Wally's clothes before settling in. The Little Drunk laughed and climbed in the passenger side.

Ruby got in and started the engine, telling her mother that she thought they were pushing it a little hard, what with the car business. Then she got to picturing Judd Gulley, hung-over and barefoot, walking up a gravel road wearing nothing but a pissy sheet and handcuffed to Wally McDonald, and she started to laugh.

"I wish I could see it, Ma, I really do."

"Well, and who says you won't? Ain't you helping with the Ladies' Auxiliary tomorrow?"

"Helping them with what?" asked Ruby.

"Tomorrow's the last Saturday in October. You know that's the day the Ladies' Auxiliary gets together to pick the trash out the ditches all along the dump road. I think maybe I'll help this year, myself."

"Pickles," said Wilson, and Ruby laughed harder.

"Pickles, it is, Wilson."

THE END

AUTHOR NOTES

When first written in 2007, the fictional versions of Ruby and her mother quickly became favorite characters on the personal blog where they were originally published, kindling a "second part" to Ruby's saga, which then turned into a third (and very likely, a fifth and sixth).

Part 2 of The Ruby Chronicles, "The Restaurant, the Romance, & the Speakeasy" will be released in paperback, and on Amazon and other digital retail sites in late 2015.

Thanks for reading!

Les Becker

ABOUT THE AUTHOR

Les Becker is a fiction writer based in Sault Ste. Marie, Ontario, CANADA. "The Waitress, the Whiskey & the Handcuffs" is her first published work.

www.ingramcontent.com/pod-product-compliance
Lightning Source LLC
Chambersburg PA
CBHW070646130626
46555CB00006B/2728